PHILADELPHIA

PHILLIES

NL
EAST

MICHAEL E. GOODMAN

1103498
4601

Published by Creative Education, Inc.

123 S. Broad Street, Mankato, Minnesota 56001

Art Director, Rita Marshall
Cover and title page design by Virginia Evans
Cover and title page illustration by Rob Day
Type set by FinalCopy Electronic Publishing
Book design by Rita Marshall

Photos by Allsport, Tom Dipace, Duomo,
Focus on Sports, National Baseball Library,
Michael Ponzini, The Sporting News, Sports
Illustrated, UPI/Bettmann, Ron Vesley and
Wide World Photos

Library of Congress Cataloging-in-Publication Data

Goodman, Michael E.

The Philadelphia Phillies / by Michael E. Goodman.
p.   cm.

Summary: A team history of the Philadelphia
Phillies, a club that has had its ups and downs but
keeps its loyal fans.

ISBN 0-88682-455-9

1. Philadelphia Phillies (Baseball team)—History—
Juvenile literature.   [1. Philadelphia Phillies (Baseball
team)—History.   2. Baseball—History.]   I. Title.

GV875.P45G66 1991   91-2483

796.357'64'0974811—dc20   CIP

THE HOME OF THE PHILLIES

Philadelphia has always been a city at the center of American history. Both the Declaration of Independence and the Constitution were signed there, and the Liberty Bell still proudly stands in downtown Philadelphia as a symbol of American freedom. The city was even the United States capital in the early days of the country.

Philadelphia has also been a central city in the development of baseball. There was a Philadelphia team—the Athletics—in the National League in its first season, 1876. And a second team formed in Philadelphia—the Phillies—has been part of the league every year since 1883.

The Phillies have had a long history but not always a successful one. The club has had its ups and downs. It

Hall of Famer Richie Ashburn is knocked down.

The Phillies, under manager Bob Ferguson, lost their first game to the Providence Grays, 4–3.

took the Phils thirty-two years to win their first pennant and ninety-seven years to win their first world championship. That might frustrate some fans, but "Philly fanatics" have remained loyal to their baseball team, win or lose. Their devotion has been rewarded in recent years, as the team has won six Eastern Division crowns, two National League pennants, and one world championship since 1975. The Phillies were one of baseball's strongest franchises in the 1970s and 1980s, and they are building for another successful decade in the 1990s.

FROM "BIG ED" TO "ALEXANDER THE GREAT"

The long history of professional baseball in Philadelphia began fittingly in 1876. That was the year that Philadelphians led the rest of the nation in celebrating the country's centennial. Residents of the City of Brotherly Love had something else to celebrate on April 22, 1876, as they watched their Athletics host the Boston Red Stockings in the first game in the history of the National League. Sadly, that first team was disbanded in midseason, and it would be seven years before Philadelphia got another National League franchise.

In 1883, a wealthy sporting goods manufacturer named Alfred Reach purchased the National League club in Worcester, Massachusetts, and moved it to Philadelphia. Reach's new Phillies had lots of fan support in their first year—but not much talent. The team won only seventeen games and lost eighty-one, and its .183 winning percentage is still the worst in club history.

Tim McCarver, a member of the Phillies during the 1970s.

Nap Lajoie became the first player in history to be intentionally walked with the bases loaded.

Better times were soon on the way. Reach brought a series of outstanding sluggers to Philadelphia over the next few years, and the team rose to near the top of the National League. No opposing pitcher wanted to face the fearsome Phillie lineup in the 1890s.

The 1894 Phillies were the most amazing team of the era. Led by future Hall of Famers Ed Delahanty, Billy Hamilton, and Sam Thompson, the club had a team batting average of .349! That's still the major league record. The Phils averaged thirteen hits a game and in one contest banged out thirty-six safeties.

Unfortunately, even with all of its sluggers, the team never quite reached the top of the National League in its early years. The problem was that Philadelphia's pitching could never match its hitting, so the club usually finished in third or fourth place.

All of that began to change in 1911, when a tall, gangly right-handed pitcher named Grover Cleveland Alexander arrived in Philadelphia. Alexander didn't look like a future Hall of Famer, but he pitched like one. "His uniform never seemed to fit properly, and his cap looked a size too small," wrote one baseball historian. "Yet his pitching motion was economical, effortless, and graceful. His control was extraordinary too. Batters who tried to wait him out for a walk, usually fanned."

The Phillies acquired Alexander from a minor league team in Syracuse, New York, for only $750. That was one of the greatest bargains in baseball history. As a rookie with the Phillies, Alexander led the National League in wins (twenty-eight), complete games (thirty-one), innings pitched (367), and shutouts (seven). And he continued to improve.

"I'd say that Alexander was the most amazing pitcher in the National League," said the legendary Casey Stengel, who faced the Phillies ace many times. "He had to pitch in that little Philadelphia park with the big tin fence in right field (only 272 feet from home plate). He pitched shutouts, which must mean he could do wondrous things with the ball. He was the best I batted against."

With one outstanding player in place, Phillie management began to look for more talent. In 1912, they added three new stars. The first was power-hitting outfielder Gavvy Kravath, who once slugged twenty-four home runs in a season—a lot in those days. The other two were catcher Bill Killefer, an excellent fielder and hitter, and left-handed pitcher Eppa Rixey, whose terrific curveball and change of pace would eventually help him enter the Hall of Fame.

Now that the Phillies had both strong hitting and strong pitching for the first time in their history, they were ready to make a run for the National League pennant. That's what happened in 1915. Alexander won thirty-one games, including twelve shutouts. Kravath led the National League in home runs and runs batted in, and first baseman Fred Luderus was second in batting average. Together, they powered the Phillies to their first National League title ever.

Despite their fine season, the Phils were no match for the Boston Red Sox and their star pitcher Babe Ruth in the 1915 World Series. But Philadelphia fans weren't disappointed. They were thrilled that they had finally tasted victory—after thirty-two frustrating years!

In both 1916 and 1917, the Phillies also had fine seasons, finishing second each time. During those years,

Woodrow Wilson's appearance at Game 2 marked the first Presidential appearance at a World Series game.

A star for today, Lenny Dykstra.

Ex-Phillie great Larry Bowa.

Philadelphia slugger Chuck Klein (right) slammed over twenty homers for the first of five consecutive seasons.

"Alexander the Great" led the way with thirty-three and then thirty victories and solidified his claim as the best pitcher of the time. However, before the 1918 season, the Phillies' owner was having money problems, so he sold his star hurler to the Chicago Cubs. The franchise did not recover from the shock of that deal for a long time. The Phils didn't have another winning season until 1932— fourteen years later—and didn't make it back to the World Series until 1950.

THE "ALL-HIT, NO-PITCH" TEAM

After Grover Cleveland Alexander left Philadelphia, the Phillies still continued to hit the ball well and with power. They scored lots of runs throughout the 1920s and 1930s. However, their pitching staff quickly went downhill. Year after year, Phils' pitchers gave up more runs than any other staff in the league, and the team usually found itself near the bottom of the standings.

The Phillies were an amazing "all-hit, no-pitch" team—especially in 1930. That was really an unusual year in the City of Brotherly Love. All eight Phillies regulars batted .280 or better, and the squad's overall batting average was .315. The club's two top sluggers, Chuck Klein and Lefty O'Doul, each hit in the .380s. Klein also smacked forty homers and fifty-nine doubles, while driving in 170 runs! With that kind of offensive showing, you would figure that the Phils would have finished high up in the league, right? Wrong! They came in dead last with a 52–102 record. The reason for their poor showing was simple: the team's pitchers gave up an average of almost seven earned runs every game—still a major league record.

1 . 9 3 3

Chuck Klein won the NL's Triple Crown and was traded by the Phillies after the season.

The Phils played some wild games in 1930. For example, during back-to-back days in July, they twice scored fifteen runs but lost both contests, 16–15 and 19–15. Sportswriter William Mead summed up the 1930 season when he noted, "For hitting, no team was the superior of the Phillies, except whomever was batting against their pitchers."

Little by little, Phillies' fans started to desert the team. Fewer fans meant less money for the team's owners, who were sinking into debt. All the club's better players—like Klein, O'Doul, Dick Bartell, Dolph Camilli, Spud Davis, and Claude Passeau—were sold or traded away for lesser players who could be paid lower salaries. Things got so bad that the league had to take over the debt-ridden team in 1943 and find new owners,

Robert Carpenter and his son Bob, Jr. They controlled the team for the next thirty-eight years and led it back to respectability.

The Phillies name was shortened to Phils at the request of manager Hans Lobert.

"THE WHIZ KIDS"

The Carpenters wasted little time getting down to rebuilding the Phillies. They hired a new general manager, Herb Pennock, and provided him with the money he needed to reestablish the club's minor league system. In just a few short years, the farm produced several outstanding talents for the big-league squad. In the middle and late 1940s, such future stars as outfielders Richie Ashburn and Del Ennis, shortstop Granny Hamner, catcher Andy Seminick, and pitchers Robin Roberts and Curt Simmons were brought up to Philadelphia.

The young, hungry Phils began a dramatic rise in the standings. They were eighth and last in 1947 but jumped to sixth in 1948 and third in 1949. Phillies' fans began calling their youthful heroes "the Whiz Kids" and dreamed of a first-place finish in 1950.

Leading the way on the 1950 team was a pair of very different pitchers—twenty-four-year-old fireballer Robin Roberts and thirty-three-year-old reliever Jim Konstanty, whose ball seemed to travel in slow motion as it headed toward the plate and then sank away from the batter.

Konstanty was one of the first relief specialists in baseball. He came in only at the end of games to try to hold a Phillies' lead or keep the game close so the Phils could come back and win. Phillies manager Eddie Sawyer seemed to call on Konstanty every other game

Like Roberts, Terry Mulholland was a fireballer.

*Like Jim Konstanty,
Del Ennis (right)
also experienced a
great season, belting
31 homers and
driving in 126 runs.*

during the 1950 season. "I could feel it coming," Konstanty said. "I would always turn to the bullpen coach and tell him to answer the telephone from the bench. He would start to tell me that the phone wasn't ringing. But, sure enough, it would go off, and I'd be heading to the mound."

Konstanty pitched in a league-leading seventy-four games that year, winning sixteen and saving twenty-two others. That was good enough to earn him the Most Valuable Player Award in the National League in 1950.

But the pitcher that manager Sawyer called on for one of the biggest games in Phillies history was Robin Roberts. The date was October 2, 1950. The Phillies were facing off against the Dodgers in Brooklyn for the last game of the season. The Phils held a slim one-game lead over the Dodgers. A Phillies win meant the team's first

The ever-hustling Pete Rose.

For the fifth consecutive season Philadelphia ace Robin Roberts led the NL in victories (23).

pennant since 1915. A loss meant the two teams would have to have a play-off for the National League title.

The game had a double importance for Roberts. He had already won nineteen games during the season, and no Phillies pitcher since Grover Cleveland Alexander (way back in 1917) had won twenty or more games in one year. Roberts wanted to join that select club.

The Phillies-Dodgers game was a titanic struggle that went into extra innings. Then Phillies first baseman Dick Sisler slammed a home run in the top of the tenth to put his team ahead, 2–1. Roberts made the lead stand up. He became a twenty-game winner for the first time, and the Phils were National League champs—finally!

As he would be all of his career, Robin Roberts had been strongest when the pressure was greatest. A team-mate once asked the Phillies' ace what special quality enabled him to win in the clutch. "It's nothing you can see," was Roberts's reply. "It comes from inside."

PITCHING AND POWER

After their 1950 title run, the Phillies sank back in the National League standings once again. Their two shining stars were Robin Roberts, who won twenty or more games for six straight seasons in the 1950s, and Richie Ashburn, whose hitting and fielding were among the best in the league.

Jim Bunning pitched the Phillies first and only perfect game on June 21.

The Phillies improved in the early 1960s and made another run for the National League pennant in 1964. They were in first place by six games with only ten games to go. Then they folded completely, to their fans' dismay, and the St. Louis Cardinals caught and passed them. That was one of the saddest times in Phillies history.

By the mid-1970s, the team was rebuilding again. New manager Danny Ozark put together a squad that combined pitching and power. The key to the pitching was Steve Carlton. "Lefty" was an intense, private person who didn't have much to say to fans or sportswriters. Instead, he let his excellent fastball and slider do all the talking for him. Those two pitches helped him win 329 games to become the only National League pitcher to receive four Cy Young Awards.

The main power source for the Phils at this time was a young third baseman named Mike Schmidt. Schmidt joined the team in 1973 and hit an impressive eighteen homers in his rookie year. Then he went on a tear. During the next fourteen seasons, he crushed thirty or

Gary Maddox.

more home runs thirteen times, led the National League in homers nine times, and drove in nearly 1,500 runs. He was also an outstanding third sacker, winning the Gold Glove award for fielding year after year.

"Mike is a professional," commented Paul Owens, one of his managers. "He plays so hard, like a man who's fighting to keep his job. Consistency is the only word you can use to describe him."

1 9 7 6

Slugger Greg Luzinski was one of five Phillies to be named to the NL's All-Star team.

Schmidt had another word to explain his success—*concentration*. "I concentrate every second I'm out on the field. For the two minutes from the time I'm on deck until the end of an at bat, no one is trying harder than I am," he said.

The Phillies of the late 1970s and early 1980s had other stars besides Carlton and Schmidt. There were starting pitchers Jim Lonborg and Jim Kaat, and relief aces Dick Ruthven, Ron Reed, and Tug McGraw. Other outstanding hitters included Greg ("The Bull") Luzinski and Gary Maddox. Among the top fielders were catcher Bob Boone and shortstop Larry Bowa. That crew powered the Phils to the head of the National League Eastern Division. Philadelphia finished atop the division three years in a row—1976, 1977, and 1978. Each time, however, the team failed to win the National League play-offs and gain a spot in the World Series.

Then, in 1979, Pete Rose moved over from Cincinnati to Philadelphia. Rose, who had been a leader of Cinci's "Big Red Machine" when it won championships in 1972, 1975, and 1976, was the missing ingredient. Some people wondered at first if Mike Schmidt and Pete Rose would be able to play together. Would they be jealous of each other's fame?

Left to right: Mike Schmidt, Tug McGraw, Steve Carlton, Bob Boone.

Phillies fans had no reason to worry. Schmidt and Rose proved to be a great duo on offense in 1980. Rose batted .282 and smacked a league-leading forty-two doubles, while Schmidt topped the National League in homers (forty-eight) and RBI (121). Meanwhile, Carlton earned another Cy Young Award with a 239 record, and McGraw saved twenty games in relief to help the Phils capture their fourth National League East title in five years.

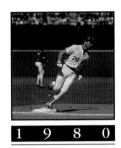

1 9 8 0

Philadelphia third baseman Mike Schmidt won the first of his three MVP awards.

Then the team began another journey toward a world's championship. The first obstacle was the National League West leader, the Houston Astros, who faced off against the Phils in the league play-offs. The Philadelphia-Houston series went five tough games—the last three into extra innings—before the Phillies won and earned a spot against the Kansas City Royals in the World Series.

Experts predicted that the 1980 Series would be a close one between two evenly matched squads. They were right. The Phils jumped out to a quick lead by winning the first two contests at home. However, the Royals quickly bounced back with wins in games three and four in Kansas City. In game five, the Phillies rallied in the top of the ninth to score the tying and winning runs. "One more victory!" Phillies fans began chanting.

The two teams returned to Philadelphia for game six. An overflow crowd packed Veterans' Stadium to see if the Phils would finally do it after ninety-seven years. Fittingly, Steve Carlton was on the mound as the game began. "Lefty" pitched seven strong innings and left the game with his team ahead, 4–0. It was up to Tug McGraw to save the win. The Royals scored once in the eighth inning and threatened in the ninth.

Outfielder Von Hayes led the team in RBI, walks, home runs, runs and total bases.

McGraw didn't make it easy for himself or the hometown fans in the last inning. He gave up two singles and a walk to put the tying runs on base with only one out. The next batter was KC's Frank White. White sent a foul ball between home and first base. Catcher Bob Boone camped under it, but the ball popped out of his glove. However, before the ball could reach the ground, Pete Rose miraculously grabbed it for the second out. "When I saw that catch," said KC star George Brett, "I knew it was over for us." Brett was right. McGraw struck out Willie Wilson to end the game.

"This is the end of an incredible journey," a joyous McGraw told reporters after the game. The Phils had traveled a long, long road to win their first world championship.

LOOKING AHEAD

Schmidt, Carlton, and Rose would be around for one more Philly pennant winner in 1983, but this time the Phils were no match for the American League champs, the Baltimore Orioles, in the World Series.

During the rest of the 1980s, Philadelphia slowly began sinking once again in the standings. The team finished in the National League East cellar in 1988 and 1989 but then began a remarkable revival in the 1990s.

The keys to the Phillies' resurgence were several controversial trades made by general manager Lee Thomas. Thomas exchanged some of the team's top veterans for a group of scrappy young players, including outfielders Lenny Dykstra and Curt Ford; pitchers Roger

Outfielder John Kruk (left) sneaks home to score the winning run in a game against the Cubs.

McDowell, Dennis Cook, and Terry Mulholland; and infielders John Kruk, Randy Ready, and Charlie Hayes. He also brought over veteran Dale Murphy, a two-time league Most Valuable Player, from Atlanta.

Some writers and fans put down the trades, but not retired Phillies star Mike Schmidt. "These guys could make a 40-year-old feel 30 again with their enthusiasm," Schmidt stated. "Sometimes I wish they could have made those trades before I retired. I might still be playing."

One player who didn't like the trades at first was Lenny Dykstra, who was unhappy moving over from the New York Mets to the Phillies. "I told him that if he didn't want to play for us, I would find him another team," said general manager Thomas. "I also told him he was the man who could turn us around."

Reliever Roger McDowell.

Third baseman Charlie Hayes.

Dykstra began doing just that with some hard hitting, daring baserunning, and exciting fielding. Lenny's nickname is "Nails" because of his "hard-as-nails" determination. He'll run through a wall to catch a flyball and do anything to get on base—slap a hit, walk, get hit by a pitch. "He has this winning glow about him that you can see even when he just walks through the clubhouse. I'm glad I don't have to play against him," said teammate Roger McDowell.

Dykstra's attitude has spread to the other young Phillies, and they have begun playing together like a team and winning. With "Nails," Murphy, and the rest of the young Phillies on board, the future looks bright for the 1990s. A new winning spirit has come to one of America's oldest and most historic cities and one of baseball's oldest franchises.